The Mystery of the Cheese

ISBN 0-7696-4041-9

School Specialty
Children's Publishing

Text Copyright © Evans Brothers Ltd. 2004. Illustration Copyright © Ruth Rivers 2004. First published by Evans Brothers Limited, 2A Portman Mansions, Chiltern Street, London W1U 6NR , United Kingdom. This edition published under license from Zero to Ten Limited. All rights reserved. Printed in China. This edition published in 2005 by Gingham Dog Press, an imprint of School Specialty Children's Publishing, a member of the School Specialty Family.

Library of Congress-in-Publication Data is on file with the publisher.

Send all inquires to:
8720 Orion Place
Columbus, OH 43240-2111

ISBN 0-7696-4041-9

1 2 3 4 5 6 7 8 9 10 EVN 10 09 08 07 06 05 04

The Mystery of the Cheese

By Paul Harrison

Illustrated by Ruth Rivers

GINGHAM DOG
PRESS

Columbus, Ohio

One night, a man was walking
along the ocean.
I wish I had some food for my hungry family,
he thought.

The man looked at the ocean.
He saw a large piece of cheese
under the water.

The man reached out.
He tried to pick up the cheese.
But the cheese moved.

So, the man waded into the water.
He reached out for the cheese.
But the cheese moved.

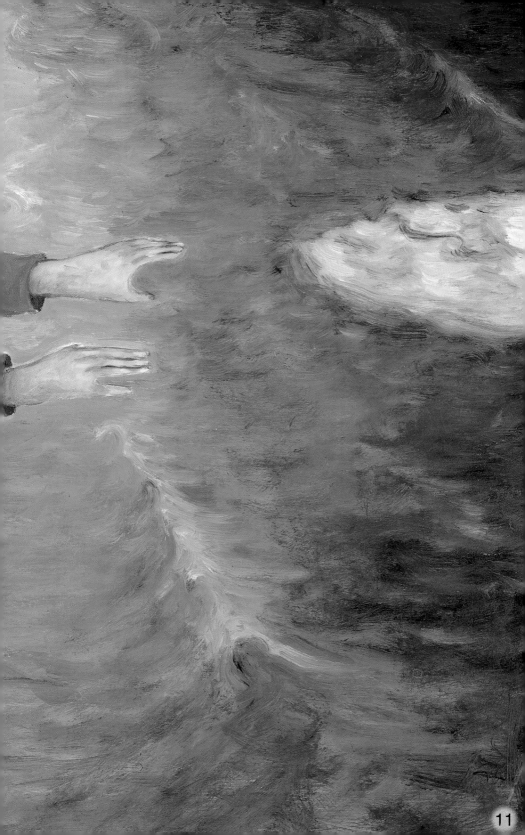

The man went home.

"Wife, there is a piece of cheese under the water," he said.
"Help me get it."

But they could not reach the cheese.

14

The man and his wife went home.

"Daughter, there is a piece of cheese
under the water," he said.
"Help me get it."

But they could not reach the cheese.

The man and his family went home.

"Dog, there is a piece of cheese under the water," he said.
"Help me get it."

But they could not reach the cheese.

We need a boat, thought the man.

So, he went home and got a boat.

They all climbed into the boat.
They chased the cheese all over
the water.

Suddenly, the sky got cloudy.
The cheese disappeared.
"That is not a piece of cheese,"
said the daughter.
"That is the moon!"

The family felt very foolish.
"Oh, well," said the father.
"I do not like cheese anyway."

Challenge Words

cheese   foolish

cloudy   waded

disappeared

Think About It!

1. What happened every time someone reached for the piece of cheese?
2. Who did the man ask to help him get the piece of cheese?
3. How did the piece of cheese disappear?
4. What did the piece of cheese turn out to be?

The Story and You

1. Why do you think the man said that he did not like cheese anyway?
2. Have you ever pretended to not want something because you could not have it?